Silly Sof

COLLEEN MAY ANDERSON

ISBN-13: 978-1544904924
ISBN-10:1544904924

DEDICATION

To my parents, for your unconditional love and support.
And to Sofie, for always making me laugh.

$\mathcal{A}$ little yellow puppy was sleeping in a sunbeam. She was dreaming about who she was.

Sofie

She liked to play with shoelaces.
Was she a kitten?

She liked to play in the mud.
Was she a pig?

She liked to play in the water.
Was she a duck?

TAP. TAP. TAP.
PEEK. PEEK. PEEK.

A black and white bird was looking through the window.

"Hello," said the bird.
"I'm a hairy woodpecker. Who are you?"

"Hello," said the puppy.
"My name is Sofie. Am I a woodpecker too?"

The woodpecker ruffled his feathers and laughed.
And laughed.
And laughed.

"Silly Sofie," he said.
"You're not a woodpecker. You're a puppy."

The woodpecker flew away.

Sofie trotted out to the garden.
There were so many flowers to smell.

CROAK. CROAK. CROAK.
RIBBIT. RIBBIT. RIBBIT.

A bright green frog was sitting on a rock.
He stuck out his long, sticky tongue and caught a
fly.

"Hello," said the frog.
"I'm a tree frog. Who are you?"

"Hello," said the puppy.
"My name is Sofie. Am I a frog too?"

The frog jumped off the rock and laughed.
And laughed.
And laughed.

"Silly Sofie," he said.
"You're not a frog. You're a puppy."

The frog hopped away.

CHATTER. CHATTER. CHATTER.
SQUEAK. SQUEAK. SQUEAK.

A fluffy red squirrel was holding an acorn in her
paws.

"Hello," said the squirrel.
"I'm a red squirrel. Who are you?"

"Hello," said the puppy.
"My name is Sofie. Am I a squirrel too?"

The squirrel flicked her bushy tail and laughed.
And laughed.
And laughed.

"Silly Sofie," she said.
"You're not a squirrel. You're a puppy."

The squirrel leapt into a tree and climbed up and away.

NIBBLE. NIBBLE. NIBBLE.
CRUNCH. CRUNCH. CRUNCH.

A large brown rabbit was eating a carrot from the garden.

Sofie's tummy grumbled. She liked carrots too.

"Hello," said the rabbit.
"I'm a Cottontail rabbit. Who are you?"

"Hello," said the puppy.
"My name is Sofie. Am I a rabbit too?"

The rabbit twitched her nose and laughed.
And laughed.
And laughed.

"Silly Sofie," she said.
"You're not a rabbit. You're a puppy."

The rabbit slipped under the fence and hopped away.

ARF. ARF. ARF.
WOOF. WOOF. WOOF.

A little grey dog was digging a hole in the garden.

"Hello," said the dog.
"I'm a puppy. Who are you?"

Sofie wagged her tail with excitement.

"My name is Sofie. And I'm a puppy too!"

ABOUT THE AUTHOR

Colleen May Anderson is a writer who lives in Toronto, Canada. She has an Honours Bachelor of Arts degree in Drama and a Bachelor of Education. After an early career as an elementary school teacher, Colleen became a technical writer. She began oil painting as a child and has worked in a variety of artistic media over the years. Colleen is an avid gardener and has a weakness for Labrador Retrievers with a sense of humour.

53315536R00020

Made in the USA
Middletown, DE
26 November 2017